The Tattoo and Body piercing Survival G

D G Jones

© 1999 Necropolis Literature

Also by D G Jones exclusive to Amazon:

THE MACHINE- Industrial Edition

THE MACHINE- Easy Read Edition

Persecution

Politically Motivated

Strange Erotica

Dave Malarkey

The Oddball Express

Lovecraft's Chip Shop

Stephen King's Trousers

Poe's Replacement

For info email: theflayedprince@yahoo.co.uk

Follow on Twitter: @theflayedprince

Website: www.theflayedprince.co.uk

Acknowledgements

The author would like to thank all friends and family, the staff and members of the Tattoo Club of Northampton, all of whom have had to put up with him for so long. Many thanks also to the army of customers and associates, among whom the author has made many friends, especially those who did not sue. Body art rules.

About the author

Mad Uncle Dave is presently working as a body piercing with the Tattoo Club of Northampton. Also a freelance writer and self-confessed sex kitten, he is currently working on his plan to become emperor of the world and/or the head coach of a Swedish netball team.

Disclaimer

This book was written and conceived for two simple reasons, to raise money for charity and to have a good laugh. In no way is it meant to represent the real world of tattooing and body piercing, or the conduct of the staff within any tattoo studio anywhere. It is hoped it will be received as it intended, i.e. a bit of a piss take and basically harmless. The great majority of tattooists and body piercers are highly respectable, professional people and no offense is intended to anyone alive or dead, or partially dead or even undead. Please note that all staff portrayed in this book are male, this is not meant to dismiss the many female tattooists and piercers working in the trade, it is mainly due to the fact that males are easier to take the piss out of. This book is a work of fiction. Mostly.

Introduction

"Should my tattoo really have the word KNOB written in the shading?"

"You tattooed me last week and my arm fell off. Is there any chance of a refund?"

Just two of the many questions posed in tattoo studios throughout the world. From its humble origins of simple, primitive artists scratching basic designs into primitive customers, the tattoo art form has come a long way in inventing electric tattoo machines. Yet to this day, this beautiful craft, along with its cousin, body piercing, remains shrouded in mystery. Is it all a world of pain, tea drinking and sexual innuendo? Yes. But there is a bit more to it. Tattooing is no longer just the realm of lorry drivers, prisoners and other such deviants, a new breed of characters have arisen, artists who experiment with their designs and their customers, taking both to their limits and also a world of pain, tea drinking and sexual innuendo.

And now dear reader, it is your turn. You want a tattoo? You want to look the business? Mean, moody, perhaps even a little dangerous? Why not throw in a quick piercing for good measure, just to show everyone you don't give a fuck what people think. You want to be radical? Outrageous? Committed? Well friend, it's no bed of roses, do or die mission or any other crappy cliché that comes along in this kind of situation.

And that's where this unique survival guide comes in.

Specifically targeted to answer all those niggling doubts, this book is all the help you need on the road to true enlightenment. This and plenty of cash. So come take a walk on the moderately wild side. And remember, as my aunty used to say, it takes pains the beautiful. In this case, lots.

A brief history of tattooing

People have been doing it for years.

A brief history of body piercing

Body piercing began as a joke that got out of hand.

10 reasons to have a tattoo

Okay, before you even get to the studio, there's going to be someone trying to talk you out of it, it'll either be your mum or your partner or some well-meaning do gooder who is supposedly looking after your interests, but is really just a pain in the arse. People can be funny about self-mutilation and you might find yourself having to try and convince them (and yourself) that is the right thing to do. But hey, do you justify everything? Do you have to justify eating a Mars bar or having a quick wank when no one else is around? No. But just in case here are 10 reasons to have a tattoo (not a wank, who needs a reason for that?)

1. It's cool.
2. It's tough.
3. You get to test your own limits.
4. You get to make a statement.
5. You're mad sunshine.
6. You have something to remember your youth by and all that entails. (Unfortunately).
7. You feel like an outlaw.
8. Not everybody is that brave.
9. Not everybody is that stupid.
10. "Fuck you, who are you to judge me?"

10 reasons people will use to talk you out of a tattoo

1. "What about when you're older?"
2. "What if you get fat/pregnant (not from the tattoo obviously) and it spreads?"
3. "What happens when you grow out of Bewitched?"
4. "Get a tattoo and I'll leave you."
5. "Get tattoo and I'll stay with you."
6. "You're mad sunshine."
7. "Look at your dad, look how miserable he is with Mungo Jerry tattooed on his chest."
8. "You'll regret it."
9. "No trust me, you'll regret it one day."
10. "Please don't do it."

10 reasons for getting a piercing

1. You can take it out.

2. It makes you look hard.

3. It makes you look like you've lived a little.

4. It doesn't hurt. Much.

5. You can thread dry spaghetti through it when you get bored.

6. Old ladies will avoid you.

7. It improves your sexual performance. (Possibly).

8. It improves your looks, or at least distracts people from the fact you are ugly.

9. It makes your genitals more interesting.

10. "Why fucking not?"

10 reasons people will use to talk you out of a piercing

1. "You'll get sacked from work." (Possibly a reason to get one).

2. You will be thrown out of your house by an enraged parent/lover.

3. It hurts.

4. "You'll get leprosy."

5. "The body piercer is probably a head case." (Probably true).

6. "It'll make you look like a curtain rail."

7. "Your tongue will go septic and fall off."

8. "You're not going to put that in my mouth/fanny/whatever."

9. "It'll catch on your teeth."

10. "You'll pass out/cry/wet yourself."

The studio

So you have ignored the namby-pamby bedwetting types and stepped into the real world, but what should the studio look like? How do you know you're in the right place? Well, the studio should be clean, well ordered and above all welcoming. The working area should be gleaming and uncluttered, all equipment held in sterile containers and on no account left lying around in a sea of dog ends and half eaten sandwiches and given a quick wipe down when someone is looking. The waiting room should be pleasant with clean floors and have a good selection of designs in books presented in an orderly cabinet. In reality however, this is not always the case as customers will usually leave the books scattered everywhere, deposit McDonald's containers under the chairs, and stick chewing gum onto the carpet. This kind of behaviour is found most distressing by the staff and will usually result in a surreptitious tenner being added to the cost of the tattoo or piercing.

The attitude of the customer

Fear usually. However, some customers can get a little overconfident until they pass out, or they can sometimes be downright aggressive. This plan can be just bravado, though it is a very foolish tactic. Treating someone badly or being rude to them when they have the power to hurt you, quite legitimately, can be viewed as a grave error of judgement. A tattoo or piercing can be as painful as you wish. Aggravate the staff at your peril and find yourself in agony. Some people though come in just asking to be hurt (rude wankers being top of the list) and usually they get their wish.

The attitude of the staff

The attitude of the staff should be friendly and helpful but often isn't. Especially if you've stuffed McDonald's cartons under your chair or messed up all the books. Usually the attitude of the staff will be forced politeness, thinly veiled contempt or bored indifference. Unless the piercer wants to get into your pants, he will be quite eager to mutilate you. As for the tattooist, his attitude depends entirely on you. You will soon discover the type of people who are dealing with by asking the most common question asked in any studio, anywhere in the world. It is the one question on every virgin's lips, and perhaps the key to the man with the machine.

Is it going to hurt?

Okay, obvious, but the answer you are given will straightaway gives an indication of the tattooist's nature. He will either:

   A. Lie.
   B. Lie partially.
   C. Be brutally honest.

Therefore his answer will be:

   A. "No, it won't hurt at all."
   B. "Well, it's a mild burning sensation."
   C. "It hurts like fuck."

By now you will know exactly how your tattooist thinks (if applicable) and how he will treat you. Often, tattooists are a long haired cheerful sort of person with a ribald sense of humour and a quiet confidence that inspires immediate trust and friendship. In no way whatsoever will your tattooist be:

   A. Power mad.
   B. A sadist.
   C. A power mad sadist.

All right, so many tattooists look like they've just stepped out of a Motorhead concert, ride a Harley-Davidson and eat live worms for a laugh, but really they are the salt of the earth, good stalwart folks with names like Baz or Gaz or something abbreviated anyway as it is easier to spell, people who, had life been kinder (and personal hygiene not a condition), would probably have gone to art college or become interior design consultants rather than fashioning entire careers out of hurting people. Like a thirteenth sign of the zodiac, tattooists are a breed of their own, they can have a tendency to be plump from sitting around swearing at people and telling highly dubious anecdotes about each other, or they are built like a brick shit house with shovels sized hands telling highly dubious anecdotes about themselves. This breed know no fear, no law other than their own, and no sentence that doesn't end without the word "tea" or "twat".

Avoid any tattooist who is:

- A. Too fat (they sweat too much).
- B. Has bad eyesight.
- C. A food encrusted beard.
- D. Has no tattoos.
- E. All of the above and/or has the shakes.

As for body piercers, put simply, body piercers are sexually deranged.

Anyway, is it going to hurt? Probably yes. But unless you are some wet behind the ears cry-baby, it's nothing you can't handle, and you don't just have to sit in the chair, say your prayers and take it, there are lots of things to do whilst being tattooed to distract yourself from the mind blurring agonies you endure. Here are a few helpful hints on how to make it through your tattooing experience:

1. Try to relax, in fact try to go limp, unconsciousness is best though you may be charged extra for wasting time or sexually assaulted by the body piercer.
2. Think of somewhere warm and sunny, take your mind away from the searing pain, and picture yourself on a sandy beach with someone attractive who is not hurting you.
3. Swear at the tattooist.
4. Swear at the person who brought you to the tattooist who now on seeing your discomfort has decided not to bother.
5. Swear at the body piercer.
6. Think of how great your tattoo will look when it is finished (hopefully).
7. Think repeatedly to yourself: fuck this hurts.
8. Pass out.

And remember no one is going to take the piss out of you, should you pass out, cry, or throw up. At least, not much.

What Sort of tattoo should I have?

A tattoo should say everything about you, it should reflect the kind of person you are and represent everything you are beneath the skin. Otherwise, go for a skull.

Size of course, is important. Not everyone wants to end up like a pair of Paisley pyjamas, and the logic usually follows that the smaller the design, the less it will hurt. This logic is unsound as it all hurts to some degree or another, so why bother lumbering yourself with some tiny doodle that will have everyone asking what the fuck is that supposed to be? Think big, be bold, go for a tattoo so huge it has to fit on to two people and only makes sense when they stand side-by-side. Remember, a tattoo is like a knob, people show more interest if you have a big one.

Whatever you choose, try to avoid having your partner's name on you. This is the kiss of death to any relationship and should be avoided at all costs if you want to stay together. Also tried to avoid stereotypical designs, break the mould, and be original, a tattoo should celebrate your uniqueness as an individual. Blokes tend to go for Taz, football badges Bulldogs etc while with girls it's flowers and little devils. Think with care, tattoos last longer than a lifetime. It will still be on your skin when you are riding a hearse, (or the body piercer is riding your corpse).

Cool tattoos

Skulls

Tribal pieces

Dragons

Skulls

Snakes

Skulls with tribal pieces

Naff tattoos

Bulldogs/flags without a skull

Nike logos

Adidas logos

Tele Tubbies

Taz

Naked women

In the quest to be original however, it is easy to go too far the other way and end up with something laughable just to be different. Anyone scanning the magazines will have seen washing machines, Coke cans and jelly babies emblazoned across someone's flesh, destined soon to be a cover-up, but there is no accounting for taste.

10 really bizarre tattoos

1. A pickled egg.
2. A London bus.
3. A portrait of Bill Clinton.
4. A cheese sandwich.
5. The Pope mooning.
6. A wicker chair.
7. The cast of Eastenders.
8. A Ford Escort.
9. An empty box.
10. Nigel Kennedy.

But whatever you choose, it is not what others think that counts, who is to dictate what is good, bad or indifferent? At the end of the day, as long as you are happy, who cares? Indulge yourself.

Tattoos and fashion

Fuck fashion, tattoos rule.

Where should I have my tattoo?

 Okay, some parts of the body are more sensitive than others and your first time it's probably better to pick a spot where it won't be too bad. Someone else is the best place, but failing that, you want somewhere with a bit of padding that is easy to show off down the pub the minute you remove the dressing. Everybody does it, posing is part of the deal. What better way to show how hard and dangerous you are than whipping out a fresh tattoo complete with the lie: "look at that, didn't hurt a bit." Mostly it's blokes who indulge in this sort of bollocks, but that's blokes all over.

 Anyway, here is a quick rundown of the best and worst places for your first tattoo:

Best place for first tattoo

Upper arm

Shoulder blade

Upper thigh

Where Mad Uncle Dave works

Worst places for first tattoo

Ribs!!!!!

Lower spine.

Elbow.

Chest/breastbone (men).

Knob (men).

Manchester airport during peak season.

Things to do while waiting to be tattooed/Pierced

For some reason, many people seem to be under the vast delusion that they can walk into a tattooist's at any time and expect to be dealt with promptly. This is indeed a delusion, sometimes due to customers coming in ten minutes before closing time, not realising the time involved in the procedure (and tea drinking). Sometimes they actually believe the staff of the tattooist's is there to serve them and not to sit around smoking endless fags, talking bollocks and tea drinking. Whatever the reason, there is usually a queue, (though this is usually the queue for the toilet) and much time will have to be spent questioning the wisdom of being there in the first place. Here are a few ideas to kill time:

1. Go through all the books looking for what you want, get the counter staff to draw it up, alter it especially to your tastes, then change your mind at the last minute and have something else.

2. Irritate the staff by leaving said books everywhere.

3. Cack your pants in terror.

4. Watch everyone else cack their pants in terror.

5. Go through all the books, find the worst tattoo available, the kind of thing only an idiot would have, then talk your best friend into having it done.

6. Insult the body piercer by making polite conversation.

7. Insult the tattooist by asking him to spell a word of more than one syllable.

8. Try unsuccessfully to chat up the best looking member of the opposite/same sex by pretending to be tough.

9. Try unsuccessfully to convince everyone else in the room that you are not frightened in the slightest by the bloodcurdling screams coming from the present customer.

10. Tell the staff of the studio that you are not happy with their attitude and being kept waiting for so long. (This is only for the criminally insane or suicidal).

11. Tell a member of staff you are a brilliant artist and want to be a tattooist.

12. Stare blankly at the walls.

13. Stare blankly at everyone else staring blankly at the walls.

14. Pretend to be related to someone famous and demand a discount.

15. Ask for a discount because someone you know once had a tattoo here.

16. Unrealistically trying convincing a member of staff to make you a cup of tea.

Waiting-room quiz

Find the letter that ends the first word and begins the second to reveal a mystery word. Once you've found it, say it to a member of staff, and see what you get.

To	( )	ant
Person	( )	go
Thor	( )	eat
Bar	( )	night

Slim   ( )   vent

Write   ( )   ate

Okay, not particularly exciting, but better than the blank wall staring game.

10 reasons a tattoo is better than sex

1. It lasts longer.
2. There's less mess to clean up.
3. Nobody has to be reassured about the size/shape of their body.
4. No one has to lie and say "I love you".
5. All the emotions are real.
6. Nobody has to fake an orgasm.
7. Nobody gets pregnant (though this cannot always be certain).
8. Nobody is paranoid about the size of the prick involved.
9. Nobody farts by accident and ruins the mood (though again not always certain).
10. Nobody gets covered in spunk.

10 reasons sex is better than a tattoo

1. The orgasm.
2. Less pain involved (usually).
3. It takes less time to learn.
4. It doesn't matter how much your hands shake.
5. The orgasm.
6. You feel less like throwing up afterwards.
7. You can switch the lights off if you or the other person is ugly.
8. You don't usually have to queue (?).
9. You don't usually have an audience (??).
10. The orgasm.

The first time

So you've waited patiently for the tattooist to finish his umpteenth cigarette washed down by yet another cup of tea. You've had all the jokes about being a virgin, about which way up you want to do it and losing your bottle. Finally, he calls you in and it's your first time in the magic chair. This is the big moment, standing on the brink (well sitting actually) of an agony greater than a Chas and Dave single. All that doubt, all that worry now washed away as the machine fires into life, the pulse quickens, the bowels loosen. But what can you expect? Here are two case studies about that crucial first time.

1. Mad Uncle Dave:

My first time was absolutely terrifying and I have to admit a bit of a disaster. I was pissed out of my head and didn't have a clue what I was doing. I won't ever forget UB40 blaring away on the stereo playing Red Red Wine and I was shaking all over. I was just worried about how fast I was going to cum, I wasn't really worried about the size of my dick having seen I was no different from the other boys at school. Anyway, I was with this fat girl who I didn't really know and she smelt a bit funny. I'd seen the movie The Thing a few nights before and when I saw her bits and pieces all those memories came flooding back and I thought to myself, you want me to put my dick into that? I think I ended up a little traumatised and that's where my interest in dead bodies comes from, that's what the therapist said. As for my first tattoo, it was a doddle. Nowhere near as scary as my first shag. I can never listen to UB40 without thinking of sweaty fat girls.

2. Claire Wright.

Personally, I was more embarrassed about my fat stomach, I had a dolphin over my belly button and it stung a little. Women take it better than blokes, so they say, and I didn't want to let the side down. Since my first I have now had three more and am completely addicted. Also, I think body piercers are the best fuck, (I'm sure I recognised the one lurking near the kettle), I love tattoos and piercings, cheap at twice the price and better than sex, although I have to say, I am a made up character and this is all complete bollocks.

10 interactive tattoos

1. A crossword puzzle.
2. A series of dots that join up in the shape of a knob.
3. A word search puzzle.
4. A paint by numbers landscape.
5. A chess board.
6. An empty noughts and crosses grid.
7. A barcode from a durex packet.
8. A magic eye portrait.
9. A plan of that maze from The Shining.
10. A series of dots that join up in the shape of a big job.

Tattoos and music

It has been argued that the music you listen to can have an influence on the kind of tattoo you have. Who gives a wank?

Body piercing-a brief introduction

Body piercing is often viewed as the poor relation of the body art community, but as this is a view held mainly by tattooists, that can be ignored from the start. Piercing is an art form just as old and just as steeped in tradition as a bunch of cave men gouging each other with burnt sticks and bone splinters. Basically, there are two branches of the art, decorative and functional (although both can be both at the same time or simultaneously, no wait that doesn't make any sense), anyway the latter usually sexually orientated. As piercing becomes more and more acceptable it is much harder to be original, but persevere, if you have the imagination, you can guarantee your body piercer will be insane enough to try it. Most piercings are relatively painless these days and some can be frozen before the procedure, technically known as 'grab it and stab it'. But don't be fooled by this term, most body piercers will have done the minutes of training after vacating whichever mental institution they have escaped from. Although, you do have to be careful, there are a few cowboys around, mostly working privately who have seen a couple of episodes of Casualty and reckon it's fun to stick sharp things into people, but it's easy to spot the class from the crap.

A good piercer will:

Be relaxed.

Be confident.

Put you at ease.

Get your piercing straight.

A good piercer won't:

Be aggressive (sometimes).

Drool.

Try to talk you into bed (if you're ugly).

Offer to show you his Prince Albert.

Body piercing is a serious business, not as some might believe a question of getting a big pointy bit of steel and hoping for the best, (though it may seem that way most of the time). It has a language all of its own and the following is a list of some of the terms commonly used:

Labret: lower lip.

Madonna's mole: upper lip, over a bit.

Septum: middle of the nose that bulls and pigs have a ring through and hurts like fuck.

Prince Albert: penis, down the Japs eye and out the bottom.

Frenum: penis, underneath, that weird stringy bit.

Ampallang: penis, straight through the helmet either horizontally or vertically, the kind of piercing you have to be out of your tree to consider.

Web: skin between fingers or any other bits.

Clithood: the hood of skin just above the clitoris which most blokes can't find.

Trig: that knobbly bit of gristle next to the ear hole.

Geish: the fold of skin between the genitals and anus. Not to be confused with a quiche, which is an egg-based flan related dish.

Bollocks: a term used by cowboy piercers, muttered under the breath meaning: "I've just fucked up piercing."

Body piercer: a social misfit who enjoys autopsies and hurting people.

Mad Uncle Dave: the top man, the geezer, the best piercer since Vlad the Impaler, though known to exaggerate. A lot.

All right, body piercers come in for a lot of stick, partially due to the nature of the business, partially due to the prejudice that still exists to those of an unstable disposition. But mainly, it's down to the social strata within the world of body art, i.e. the fact that tattooists expect the piercer to make the tea all the time, which is outrageous. But at the end of the day most are genuine artists with a love of their art form. They are knockabout people with a good sense of humour, usually well-endowed and fantastic in bed, but this might be another exaggeration. Don't knock your piercer, especially if he has a cup of tea or a needle in his hand, they are a revelation and much better than tattooists. However, if they list their three favourite films as Hellraiser, Driller Killer and the Texas Chainsaw Massacre, forget it.

10 reasons a tattoo is bad

1. The tattooist was crap.
2. The tattooist was still in the process of learning to tattoo.
3. The tattooist didn't like you.
4. The design was bad.
5. The design was too difficult.
6. The design was under-priced and too difficult therefore hurried.
7. The tattooist was in a bad mood/hung over.
8. You shook too much.
9. The tattooist shook too much.
10. You were too sweaty and the tattooist didn't want to hang around.

10 excuses for a bad tattoo

1. "You moved and the lines went wobbly."
2. "You have bad skin."
3. "You moved and have bad skin."
4. "That's not my work."
5. "The lines broke up because you picked it."
6. "Something must have been rubbing on it."

7. "You've been on a sunbed."
8. "You've been soaking in the bath."
9. "You have leprosy."
10. "Fuck off."

10 reasons your piercing is bad

1. The body piercer.
2. The body piercer showed up.
3. The body piercer showed up and didn't want to shag you.
4. The piercing hadn't been done before.
5. The body piercer didn't want to shag you or the mate you brought along for moral support.
6. The body piercer kept looking at your tits.
7. The body piercer was distracted by someone else's tits.
8. Chas and Dave were on the radio at the time.
9. The body piercer was too pissed to see straight.
10. The body piercer didn't like you and wanted you to have a crap piercing.

10 excuses for a bad piercing

1. "Well, the piercing is straight, but your body isn't, try walking around at an angle."

2. "You moved."
3. "The clamps were damaged and twisted your skin."
4. "You're too fat."
5. "You're too thin."
6. "The needle was crooked."
7. "You screamed when I started and put me off."
8. "You're a wanker."
9. "Fuck off."
10. "Never mind the piercing darling, what's your phone number?"

Tattoos and the media

Tattoos have a bad press, of this there can be little or no doubt. Recently, a story in the papers commented on a "Tattooed Cannibal Killer", that bloke who ate his girlfriend. If he had had no tattoos, would they have said: "Untattooed Cannibal Killer"? No. For some reason, there is still a popular belief among the press organisations that getting a tattoo will prove you are a dangerous, bloodthirsty maniac. Sounds like the perfect excuse to get one.

Are there any risks from getting a tattoo?

As long as all the equipment is sterile, and the tattooist is a professional, there are no risks. All studios have to pass rigorous inspections and display a copy of the appropriate bylaws. The only risk from a tattoo is being bored to death while waiting for the tea drinking and fag smoking to stop.

Are there any risks from getting a piercing?

Again, all hygiene standards have to be observed in a studio, however there are those who practice the art at home only just having decided to give it a go so be careful. Some piercings are a little riskier and these risks will be explained to you by the piercer, unless of course, he doesn't like you. You only have one body, so see a profession. Usually though, the only risk from a piercing is if you upset the body piercer, then he may well decide to pierce your Prince Albert with a set of darts from across the room, or accidentally on purpose slip with the needle and stick it through your eyeball.

Are there any risks from the customers?

Yes.

Good customers

1. Ones who sit still.
2. Have proper money.
3. Don't mind waiting.
4. Don't mind nipping to the shops for a pint of milk and 20 Embassy.
5. Ones who put the books back properly.
6. Ones who don't moan when you fuck up their nervous system.

Bad customers

1. Ones who mess up the books.
2. Ones who argue over the price.
3. Ones who squirm all over the place.
4. Drunks who believe they will be tattooed.
5. Wankers who complain if you fuck up their nervous system/skin/piercing/tattoo/life.
6. Ones who are in the studio because it's raining, with no intention of having anything, who mess up the books while pretending to look for a suitable design then piss off when the sun comes out and/or their bus is due.

10 ways the staff will get their own back on you if you upset them

Being a temperamental lot, it's easy to upset the staff of a tattoo studio. They can and will take their revenge, don't doubt it for a second.

1. The tattooist will lean the machine into you as hard as possible.
2. The body piercer will change the direction of the piercing whilst the needle is still in your flesh.
3. The tattoo you wanted of that loved one will end up cross eyed.
4. Your Taz will include added genitalia.
5. The body piercer will accidentally clamp you so hard they have to peel you off the ceiling.
6. The body piercer will tell you some fictitious, but plausible horror story about the piercing you have just had.
7. The tattooist will put the name of someone else in the scroll you've just asked to include your partner's name. (He may also deliberately spell it wrong, but this is not usually deliberate).
8. Whilst being tattooed, the staff will engage in a conversation so disgusting that if you didn't feel like throwing up before, you soon will.

9. The body piercer will inform you that the Japanese symbol you just had actually means twat in Japanese.
10. Your tattoo contains the word knob surreptitiously hidden in the shading.

How much is this tattoo?

A very common question as tattoo designs are never usually priced up in the studio. This is because no one can be bothered to do it and prices are usually made up on the spot. Never ask for a price over the phone, never ask for a price if the tattoo has just spilt his tea. Tattoo prices are usually judged on how long they will take to do, supposedly, so detail and size are important. Also the customer's attitude, any imminent bills facing the studio or a lack of tea and nicotine are all deciding factors, the answer in these circumstances usually being: "fucking dear."

How long will my tattoo/piercing take to heal?

How long is a dog's knob? Who knows? Usually tattoo's take 7 to 10 days, whilst with piercings it's 4 to 6 weeks. Most are guaranteed, until you've left the building. After you've paid, who cares?

How do I look after my tattoo/piercing?

You will receive a full rundown of instructions from the professionals, (not Bodie and Doyle), though don't count on it if you're one of those awkward types people can't wait to be rid of. The best way to treat tattoo or a piercing is to take it out for a nice meal, somewhere expensive, preferably with Mad Uncle Dave, and afterwards give him a damn good seeing to. (If you're female that is, if you're a bloke forget it unless you bring cash).

Care of your new tattoo

Do:

Keep the dressing on for 2 to 3 hours.

Wash it, pat it dry.

Apply Savlon cream or E45.

Keep it covered from sunlight whilst healing.

Take it on holiday.

Don't:

Pick the scabs.

Soak in the bath.

Smear it with fish and chips.

Apply battery acid.

Care of your new piercing

Do:

Bathe it with dilute salt water.

Keep the dressing on (if any) for 2 to 3 hours.

Use zinc supplement tablets.

Clean jewellery before rotating it.

Don't:

Touch jewellery with dirty hands.

Fiddle about with it until it heals.

Bathe it with salt and vinegar.

Attach a Ford transit to nipple rings.

10 tattoos just for your lover

1. A suggestive banana and two cherries.
2. A suggestive cherry and two bananas (?).
3. "Insert knob here."
4. "Crank by hand only."
5. "No entry to tradesmen."
6. A smiley face.
7. "Hand wash only."
8. A London underground sign.
9. A trombone.
10. Two pickled onions and a suggestive piece of cheese.

Really dumb questions and answers

For some reason, when it comes to tattoo studios, people ask some pretty dumb questions, a personal favourite being when someone phones up and says: "is that the tattoo place, do you do tattoos?" It would be nice to believe that such questions derive from people being ill informed about the business, not because they are mentally challenged in some way.

Question: Is it going to bleed?

(Always a favourite this one, obviously not thought out all that well).

Answer: We're talking needles in skin here. What do you reckon?

Question: Do you use sterile equipment?

(This is perhaps the dumbest question of the lot, everything in a studio, except the staff, is usually sterile. Be warned people can get pregnant just by shaking hands with a tattooist).

Answer: No, we've been using the same needles since 1975 and just run them under the tap a couple of times.

Question: How much will a tattoo about this big cost?

(This question is usually accompanied with a vague hand gesture or asked over the phone. It is guaranteed to piss off the respondent).

Answer: How the fuck am I supposed to know, you could be talking about anything. Fuck off and get a fucking life.

Question: Have you ever tattooed/pierced a bloke's dick?

(This question is very popular and people are always fascinated with this small part of the trade, the colder weather the smaller the part. Everyone has heard of someone, somewhere who has had it done, usually some fuckwit in a pub who's pissed out of his head and wants to show you. That or a body piercer. And almost everyone has heard the tale about the bloke who wanted a spider tattooed on his knob which only has six legs because he couldn't take any more. This area of the business does not deserve this huge amount of limelight it receives as it doesn't happen all that often on the tattooing side of things. Blokes are usually too chicken and it's hard to find designs that small when the average penis shrivels under the machine. Prince Alberts are more common however, though one gentleman did come in and ask for a King Arthur. And also, for some reason, tattooists and piercers seem to think that if they tell people they touched another man's genitals, then they will automatically leap to the conclusion they are gay. Because the business is male dominated much of the time (which is a shame because fem dom is such fun), there is a lot of testosterone around. Mention latent homosexuality and see what you get. Sad really, but the answer always has an added justification).

Answer: Yes I have, but I'm heterosexual, honest.

Question: Have you ever tattooed/pierced a bird's fanny?

(This question usually comes from some feeble minded bloke who has all the social skill of a retarded warthog and who is trying to put a bit of sparkle into his desperately sad life. The answer of course is determined by the surrounding company and can be one of three depending if: 1. The tattooists/piercer's girlfriend is around, 2. The shop is a girlfriend free zone or 3. There are female customers present, so the answer will be as follows).

Answer one: No certainly not, what sort of disgusting question is that?

Answer two: Oh yes mate, loads and loads, never stops, day in day out.

Answer three: Occasionally but it's not as exciting as you think.

Only the last answer is anywhere near the truth, but this intriguing example hints at one of the major activities in a tattoo studio.

Bullshit

Like all other testosterone dominated industries, bullshit is a way of life and the world of body art is no exception. In fact the opposite is true, it is a shining example of such and the amount of bollocks talked in a tattoo studio is phenomenal, and it comes from all sides. On no account should you believe anything anyone says in a studio, unless you were there at the time, have a signed confession and have video evidence. Certainly in the real world everyone likes to impress and pretends to be someone important, but on this strange and confined stage, the emphasis is greater and the bullshit so more fluent, everyone has to try and out do each other with stories so outrageous, claims and anecdotes so ludicrous that if they were to be uttered outside the door, they would be considered complete crap.

Bullshit you can expect from a tattooist

1. "I learned to tattoo in prison, while I was serving a stretch for multiple murder."
2. "I have a Harley Davidson you know, 20,000cc with electro glide, soft tail and a built-in fridge."
3. "I learned to tattoo in Japan when I was a member of the Yakuza."
4. "No, we have several shops, all over Europe and a couple in America, where we are members of the Senate, and have never been prosecuted, been going years, I've been in the business since I was five but I was born with a tattoo machine in my hand."
5. "No, you see so many naked women in the end it doesn't bother you. I never letch over the customers."

6. "Tattooists make the best lovers."
7. "I have a 12 inch penis."
8. "No, I've had loads of good looking women, I just like ugly birds."
9. "I can do martial arts you know and I can kill you just by blinking my eyelids in a violent manner."
10. "No, of course it won't hurt."
11. "I once had an audition for Stars in Their Eyes."
12. "I have lots of qualifications but decided not to follow an academic career because of my disillusionment with the educational establishment."
13. "Of course I can spell."
14. "No, I'm not married."
15. "I was in the SAS and took part in several suicide missions."
16. "No, I don't ever rubbished the work of another tattooist, each to their own I say."
17. "No I'm not pissed."
18. "Yeah I once tattooed someone famous, let me see, there was Freddie Starr, Ozzy Osbourne, Melvyn Bragg, Princess Anne..."
19. "No sex for 72 hours after having a tattoo, unless it's with a registered tattooist."
20. "If you lose any colour, providing you haven't picked it, we will be happy to touch it up for you free any time."

Bullshit you can expect from a body piercer

1. "No, I won't hurt you."
2. "I have been rehabilitated into the community."
3. "I have never had sex with a corpse."
4. "I have never had sex."
5. "I have a 14 inch penis."
6. "I am actually a very gentle person."
7. "No I don't practice sadomasochism."
8. "No I don't like hurting people."
9. "I do not have a history of mental instability."
10. "I hate genital piercing."
11. "I used to be a doctor."
12. "I wasn't looking at your tits."
13. "I am a very popular person, not a social misfit."
14. "I used to be a vet."
15. "I have never been violent."
16. "Yeah I have loads of girlfriends."
17. "No, I am single, honest."
18. "No, I don't chat up every customer who comes in here, you're just very special."
19. "No, that bulge in my pocket is just my keys."
20. "Of course I know what I'm doing."

Bullshit you can expect from a customer

1. "No, I'm not scared."
2. "It was the heat that made me faint."
3. "I could sit here taking this all day."
4. "No, I'm all right."
5. "Really, what an interesting anecdote."
6. "No I won't pick the scabs off."
7. "No I didn't throw up in the toilet."
8. "Of course I trust you."
9. "No, the price is fine."
10. "Yeah I'll come in and have it finished in a couple weeks."
11. "I've shagged loads of women."
12. "I've shagged loads of blokes."
13. "No, I don't think you're a demented, sadistic bastard."
14. "I'll drop that tenner in next week."
15. "No, I didn't mind waiting three hours."
16. "I didn't mess up your books honestly... No please stop that hurts... Please..."
17. "Yeah I've got a Harley Davidson myself."
18. "No, it's true love, we are going to get married, so I will be keeping that name on me forever."

19. "I beat up six blokes in a nightclub last week, right fucking bundle it was, but I took them all on and won. Weren't you there blinking violently in the corner?"
20. "No I'm not an estate agent/accountant/sales rep/sad nobody, I'm just a member of the SAS currently on another suicide mission."

Jokes played on the customer

1. The price.
2. When the customer is having their first tattoo, the tattooist may ask them to put on a pair of surgical gloves for so-called hygiene reasons, but basically this is just a ploy to make them sit there like a twat with a pair of latex gloves on.
3. When about to perform a piercing, the body piercer may turn to the tattooist and say: "how do you do this again?"
4. When about perform a genital piercing the piercer may turn round to the tattooist and say: "hey, do you want to watch me do my first fanny/dick piercing?"
5. The tattooist may hold the machine to the customer's arm without a needle loaded into it and make out he has started. When the customer says: "that doesn't hurt a bit," he will stop, load a needle and then start, usually making the customer faint.

6. The body piercer will make the tattooist's customer a cup of tea and then put it just out of hands reach.
7. The tattooist will mutter, tut and shake his head at the fresh piercing that has just been done until the customer panics and asks what's wrong with it.
8. The body piercer will spray water on to his customer instead of freeze spray then laugh hysterically when they suffer unendurable agony.

Styles- tattoos

Henna tattoos

A complete rip-off for people who can't take the real thing and deserve to be conned.

Temporary tattoos

Everyone is talking lately about these tattoos that only lasts 3 to 5 years. Any unscrupulous tattooist will say they can be done and when you come back in five years mention: "sorry mate, used the wrong inks." Why bother getting it done? You walk around for X amount of years then suddenly decide you don't want one of your legs.

Japanese symbols

Many people enter a tattoo studio and ask if there is a Japanese alphabet available, and of course there is, in Japan. Few realise most tattooists have trouble with the English alphabet. But does your symbol actually mean what it is supposed? Possibly, maybe, unless the design has surreptitiously been altered in some way by a member of staff and that character meaning love now means wanker. But even more puzzling is the question do Japanese people have English letters tattooed on them? Do blokes proudly walk around Tokyo with the word flatulence tattooed on them? This remains a mystery.

Tribal and black work

Does it mean anything? Probably not. It's just a series of ambiguous black squiggles.

Celtic knot work

Complex interlocking squiggles that still doesn't mean anything and are fucking hard to do.

Styles- piercings

Which side?

At school, everyone hears that crap about having your ear pierced on one side or the other means you are gay or straight, and this myth has carried on into the world of body piercing. People still ask which side they should have their eyebrow or nipple ring. Does this mean all your body jewellery has to go down one side of your body? What if you have the eyebrow on the left and the nipple on the right (not literally unless you have a very strange genetic make-up or are one of those mutant types that come in from time to time), does it mean you are bisexual or simply wavering? In short, the answer is no. This myth is bollocks. Usually you can tell if someone is gay if they have relationships with partners of the same sex, and strangely enough, straight if they have relationships with members of the opposite sex. Not that it matters to anyone and is certainly not going to be dictated by which side their ear has a ring in it.

Gold or steel?

Can you pierce with gold? Yes if you have the cash. And you don't mind the jewellery tarnishing and going black. The choice of metal can be determined by personal taste, previous experience or more commonly, the cost. In the world of sadomasochism however, it is believed that doms have their genitals pierced with gold and subs with steel. Many people will approach a body piercer asking if they have a small gold ring, and this is usually confirmed or denied by their partner.

Bar or ring?

Again, this is a matter of personal choice, but a bar will usually sit straighter, flush to the body and is less likely to catch on the clothing or teeth of a rampant partner. Rings on the other hand are cheaper. Ask a piercer if they have a cheap ring and this again will be confirmed or denied by their partner.

10 amusing tattoos just for the coroner

Imagine the scene at your autopsy when they strip you off and find some flippant message tucked away in a body crevice. Have the last laugh and show you don't give a fuck.

1. "This way up."
2. "Suitable for vegetarians."
3. "Suitable for home freezing."
4. "Best before August 99."
5. "Contains flammable gas under pressure."
6. "Insert 2X9v batteries."
7. "No sex please, I'm dead."

8. "Tobacco seriously damages your health."
9. "Copyright God industries."
10. "Please recycle."

The truth about genital and sexual piercings

Genital piercing is becoming ever more popular, up and down the country people are walking into tattooists and asking to have a big needle stuck through their bits. For many, this will seem a little odd, so the first question has to be why? What would possess someone to have a complete stranger stab their joy division with a sharp piece of steel?

Well, there are many reasons, not all of them sane apparently, first and foremost people have the belief that having jewellery stuck through them will improve their performance in the sack. Is this bad technique down to feelings of inadequacy? Does this mean that blokes only get a Prince Albert or am Ampallang because they have a small willy? There is definitely a small willy thing going on here, but it is not always the case. Sometimes blokes like to decorate the above average todger to show it off, and this is often the real reason a lot of blokes get it done, so they can flop it out in a pub and say: "hey darling, take a butchers at that."

Women on the other hand get pierced downstairs for one of two reasons, one, hoping it will compensate for their partner's bad technique, (todgers aside big or small), and two, for decoration. Women sometimes like to celebrate the beauty of their body and it can be argued that a ring through the flaps is a saucy bit of kit, whilst a ring through the clit is great on bus rides.

Another often overlooked reason for genital piercing is an interest in sadomasochistic practices, and this is no bad thing, so it's best to leave that argument there.

But how functional is it? Well frenums were initially conceived to aid erection, a small metal ring jammed around the penis will restrict the blood flow and maintain erection (apparently). A clit hood piercing should allow the ring to sit on the clitoris and give it a quick tickle every now and then.

But is it safe? A lot of crap is talked about genital piercing, particularly with reference to its safety elements. In men, as long as the piercing is kept away from any main veins, genital piercing is safe (ish). In women, vaginal lip and clit hood piercings are usually safe, but piercing the actual clitoris self however can be a bit dodgy as hammering a piece of steel through a bundle of nerves can offer a 50-50 chance of desensitising it. Best stick with the hood as it does the same job with little risk. Remember, a bird in the hand is worth a ring in the bush. So how is it done?

Typical genital piercing experience-male

The customer will shuffle nervously, usually egged on by a sadistic girlfriend, or half a dozen piss taking makes who are all glad it isn't them. Usually he will whisper something about having his dick pierced, or some other childish euphemism and stand around sweating a lot. For a Prince Albert a ring large enough to account for any swelling (i.e. a stiffy) is to be selected, and sometimes the customer has to go off for a quick wank whilst measuring the distance between the japs eye and a frenum (this doesn't need to be done, but the staff think it's funny and everyone knows what he's up to in the toilet). Then comes the needle. A fucking huge needle. This is the moment of truth. The bloke will either lose his bottle and run or go through with it. If so, it's time to get his knob out, and many blokes such as rugby players love getting their knobs out (as previously discussed this is usually the motivating factor). This is nothing to be proud of and the knob isn't usually either.

Now is the time for the shrivelling to begin and is quite amazing how much a bloke's dick can shrink at the sight of the cold steel. Not surprising really considering the needle actually cores out the flesh to make room for the ring, and as the catheter is threaded down the eye, the average penis will shrink down the size of an acorn. The needle passes downwards, through a thin layer of skin and out underneath, this should be quite painless operation, though that wouldn't seem the case as the customer usually gives out a short breathless yelp. The jewellery is then threaded through the catheter and snapped shut with the ball. For polite customers, great care has been taken to grease the needle on its way down the urethra to ease the suffering, which the accompanying girlfriend has come to see. It is alarming how much pleasure they get from watching their bloke squirm, standing right over the action area with shiny eyes and a cruel grin. Particularly if they have had blokes children. The whole procedure is very quick, just very unpleasant for all involved. Never offend the piercer before having this one done. Never. Never. Never.

Typical genital piercing-female

This scenario is just as disturbing as a male genital piercing to anyone in their right mind, especially on a hot day. The customer will often come with her mind already set on having it done though a little more modest than the blokes, and is usually hesitant about getting her kit off. Many men think this must be a great thrill for the piercer, but it isn't, unless they are a real weirdo or have never seen a naked woman before. If she is having a clit hood piercing, which is the most common, the needle passes either vertically or horizontally through the hood, and again this is only a thin sliver of flesh. However, this is painful, but only sharp for a couple of seconds. If done correctly and judged carefully by the piercer, the ball of the ring should sit upon the clitoris. The customer will naturally feel very vulnerable at this point and it is best to put her at her ease straight away, and some piercers do this by pretending to be homosexual.

Women however, handled the whole procedure much better than blokes, despite a little embarrassment. They do not whimper and whine and make a complete song and dance about the whole thing. This is because most women are harder than blokes, have a higher pain threshold and a stronger will. No bad thing, as the world needs strong women, preferably ones with whips and 6 inch stilettos.

Genital horror stories

1. The woman who came in on a hot summer's day and had a fanny held together like Velcro.
2. The bloke who came in for Prince Albert with a dick so small it was like piercing a button mushroom. Worse still, the fact he was so incredibly fat it looked like a button mushroom growing out of the side of a pink hill.
3. The woman who tensed up when she was having her hood done, so much so she broke wind incredibly loudly when the needle went through.

4. The woman who came in and took down her pants to reveal a set of fresh, thick skid marks.
5. The woman who leapt so high in the air, she actually leapt off the needle.
6. The bloke who came in who hadn't bothered to take a shower beforehand, giving off that distinct and rather unpleasant aroma of Betty Swollocks
7. The woman who pissed herself.
8. The bloke who couldn't have his Prince Albert done because he kept getting a stiffy.
9. The bloke who had pierced his own dick with a padlock and it had gone septic (his dick that is not the padlock).
10. That woman who had a fungal infection and it looked like she had poured a tub of cottage cheese into her knickers.

Pushchairs

Walk into any tattoo studio, and there's usually someone with a pushchair, complete with screaming brat. This is not the kind of place to bring a buggy or a screaming brat and many tattooists and piercers will comment loudly on this, through gritted teeth on most occasions. Although this is unavoidable sometimes, it is just bloody annoying.

Scratchers

Apart from people with a venereal disease, this is a term used by professional tattooists to describe amateurs. Many people make the mistake of going to see a scratcher because they are cheap. When it is healed they have to go and have a proper tattoo to cover it, or wander around under the delusion that it is a quality piece of work. Some may politely agree with them, nodding and smiling whilst thinking how awful it is, whereas tattooists will just laugh and say: "what a load of wank that is."

Hangers on

Have you ever noticed when you're being mutilated how many people are sitting around to watch? For some strange reason tattoo studios seem to be a magnet for people with nothing better to do than hang around all day, getting in the way, talking bollocks and dropping unsubtle hints about having a cup of tea. It is perhaps a unique phenomenon, after all, you don't see people lounging around the checkouts at Sainsbury's talking a load of crap with the staff and/or making lewd comments about the size of every female customer's breasts. For some reason this uninvited audience constantly take the piss out of a customer's body, choice of design or pain tolerance and it can be extremely off-putting. But this attention can also be unwelcome by those trying to work, who do not need the added demands for tea and mindless chitchat. Who are these people, and why do some of them spend so much time being such a pain in the arse?

The tattooist's mates

These people knew the tattooists when he first started working in his kitchen and have been subjected to his very early, loosely termed "experimental" tattoos. Boy will they let you know it. They sit around talking about the old days, for some reason believing they have a God-given right to a cup of tea. They supposedly know everything there is to know about tattoos though have never actually done it and always complain about some piece of work that has never been finished or covered up. They use lines such as:

"See this, this was one of his first bits of work when I was only fifteen..."

"Do you remember when you opened your first shop and on the first day we had to..."

"I knew him when he started working from home and was charging 50p for a tattoo..."

These and other lines of no interest are the standard stock of such people, many of whom like to bask in the success and notoriety of someone else because they have done nothing special with their own lives.

Tea rating: 3 cups per visit.

The people who want to be the tattooists mates

These people try to get their feet under the table for a number of reasons, it might be for a fleeting taste of glory, knowing someone in such a glamorous business, it might be in the hope of getting some free or cut-price work every now and then, or even in the brave hope of getting the chance to work in the shop under the mistaken belief that tattooing actually pays well. Some, however, actually like the tattooist, his ribald humour, dubious anecdotes and obviously want a quick cup of tea. Some of these can be really nice people, though often, usually they are sitting around waiting and hoping to catch a glimpse of a pair of tits.

Tea rating: 1-2 cups per visit.

The body piercer's mates.

He doesn't have any. Not living ones anyway.

Tea rating: N/A

People who like body art

These people are rare, and are genuinely interested in the business as a whole. They often have a tattoo mag tucked under one arm and will talk endlessly about the latest styles and ideas around the world which will either confuse or alarm the tattooist.

Tea rating: 0-1 cups per visit

People who like talking bollocks

Let's face it, they're in the right place.

Tea rating: 1-2 cups per visit

People who wish to learn tattooing

There are lots of these and unless they have a huge wad of cash or a big pair of tits, they are ignored until they go away.

Tea rating: 0 cups per visit.

People who wish to learn body piercing

Wild eyed lunatics who foam a lot and have a deep-seated hatred of anything living that will not shag them. Or anything dead for that matter. Rare as most are confined somewhere for the safety of the public.

Tea rating: 0 cups per visit.

People with nothing better to do and have a couple of tattoos

These are the most frequent and probably the most annoying. Because they like to hang around, killing time while the wife or partner is doing the rounds at Tesco's without any help. Sometimes hinting at cheap work and certainly on the lookout for a brief glimpse of tits to brighten up their day, these people are those trying to become the tattooists mates but will never get that far, no matter how much tea they drink. They have no aspirations to learn the trade, but will talk the same amount of crap about it as everyone else.

Tea rating: 3-4 cups per visit.

Tattooing and the law

Lots of policemen have tattoos, apart from that, the law knows nothing about anything, particularly who broke into Mad Uncle Dave's car last week. If your partner has an affair that's perfectly legal, you stick a claw hammer through their head and they call it murder, where's the justice in that? Forget the law, get tattooed and become an anarchist.

Branding and scarification

Not allowed but who cares? Warm up the soldering iron and break out the scalpels.

10 things to say when your tattoo is finished

1. "Thanks fuck for that."
2. "I'm never having another one."
3. "Which hospital is this?"
4. "These are not the trousers I came in with."
5. "It's upside down."
6. "Is that how you spell Aston Villa?"
7. "Where's my watch gone?"
8. "Thanks for hurting me."
9. "How long before the bleeding stops?"
10. "Okay, a jokes a joke, please untie me."

How do I get into this business?

People want to work in this fun exciting and why not? But you have to be rich or lucky, that or shagging a tattooist in the hope that they will train you (they always make that promise). Seriously though, the tattooing/piercing business is massive, it creates a lot of jobs and pays a lot of taxes. But this doesn't stop society looking down its nose at the trade, and it's not given enough credence by the employment community at large. A good job really, otherwise everyone would be doing it and those already there wouldn't (if that makes any sense). But there is not enough help available for people, certainly not in the way of grants and subsidies to help those with a genuine passion for the work. Some form of sponsoring would help.

Many people come into the studio and ask: "how do I get into this business?" Whilst many people in the business ask: "how do I get out of it?" But once it's in your system, it's there for good, the pain, the ink, it gets into your blood and in all honesty it's one of the best jobs in the world. Where else do people come in, get hurt, then hand over money and say thank you? Apart from Madame Stella's leather dungeon, not many places at all.

Is it addictive?

Yep.

Is there any cure?

Nope. Apart from having no cash.

Final word

Okay, we've had a good time, a few laughs and a couple of gentle (?) well-meant jovial type insults (by reading this far you've agreed not to sue). But that really sums up the attitude of a tattoo studio, the whole process is a magical larger-than-life adventure and the business littered with plenty of characters and the occasional hard working person. You try taking life seriously when you have someone else's dick in your hand and a needle you could knit jumpers with.

The most important thing to remember is that it is you the customer who makes it what it is. You and your cash. Don't be afraid of your local tattoo studio, go in, have a look round without messing up the books and sample that strange, intoxicating atmosphere of blood sweat and tea. Spend your money willingly, knowing that most tattooists and piercers are warm friendly folk, dedicated to their art and working for the love of it. Certainly there's a couple of quid to be made here and there, but that is not what drives the majority into this line of work. These people are artists and skin is their canvas.

So the final word is this: there are two kinds of people in the world when it comes to tattooing and body piercing, those who talk about getting them done and those who have them. Do it today!